Once upon a time,
there were two
house cats named
Maru and Hugh.

They were living happily with a lovely girl in a cozy home.

Maru is a curious
and playful cat,

Hugh is calm and gentle,

making him absolutely lovable.

"Hugh, Let's go play
outside."

"Hmm... It might be unsafe out there."

Maru always looked
out the window

and wanted to go outside.

One day,
Maru decided to
leave the house and
find a new friend.

Worried about Maru, Hugh decided to go along.

Maru and Hugh followed a butterfly into the forest.

The forest was beautiful. However,

As it got darker,
it became a little
scary.

Well... actually, not a little, but a lot.

At that moment,
a black dog appeared
from somewhere

**and came running,
barking loudly.**

Maru and Hugh were really scared and ran away fast.

"Quick, Maru! Climb up the tree now!"

Maru was really scared, but with Hugh's help, he climbed up a tree to stay safe.

The sky from the top of the tree was really beautiful.

The trees were safe, but the birds were so noisy

that Maru and Hugh
couldn't stay long.

"Let's go back now,
Maru."

Finally, they met
other cats

but they weren't friendly and asked them to leave.

The other cats were also the same.

Maru felt deeply disappointed

Maru and Hugh were very hungry, but there was nothing to eat.

Maru and Hugh
got lost.
They didn't know
where to go.

They were cold and hungry, but they relied on each other to sleep.

That day, Hugh had
a dream of running
around like Maru.

Maru dreamed of being loved like Hugh.

On the other hand, the girl who lost her cat was very sad and searched all around.

At night, she always prayed to meet her cat friends again.

The girl promised to play with Mary and Hugh more often when she found them.

Missed those moments we spent together so much.

Thankfully, the girl finally found Maru and Hugh.

Maru and Hugh,
who met the girl,
were really happy.

Maru and Hugh
were full

and fell asleep
in a warm home.

**Maru and Hugh
were so happy
to be together.**

Well... Now, Hugh keeps going out and telling me to have fun.

도서명

Maru & Hugh

발 행 | 2023년 08월 16일

저 자 | 채영란

펴낸이 | 한건희

펴낸곳 | 주식회사 부크크

출판사등록 | 2014.07.15.(제2014-16호)

주 소 | 서울특별시 금천구 가산디지털1로 119 SK트윈타워 A동 305호

전 화 | 1670-8316

이메일 | info@bookk.co.kr

ISBN | 979-11-410-4005-5

www.bookk.co.kr